LEPRECHAUN vs.

By Todd Tarpley

Illustrated by Stephanie Laberis

EASTER BUNNY

L B

Little, Brown and Company
New York Boston

High on the hill
where the clover is green,
and rainbows are brighter
than you've ever seen...

. . . a wee little leprechaun
popped up his head.
"'Tis the spot I shall bury
my treasure!" he said.

"Now, hold on there, buster," a brown bunny shouted. "You're digging where all of my tulips have sprouted!

"It's the perfect location
for hiding my eggs.

"So get off my lawn
with your scrawny green legs!"

The leprechaun bellowed,
"You're in for a fight!
You picked the wrong guy!"
And guess what? He was right.

He sprinkled some shiny gold
coins on the ground,
then hid near a tree
till the bunny came round.

"Gold!" cried the bunny, but when he bent over, the leprechaun pushed him facedown in the clover!

The bunny got up
and, boy, was he mad!
He stomped and he scowled
and he growled, I might add.

"A bunny like me,
we hide things in the lawn—
like this gadget I like to call
Leprechaun Gone!"

Now, can leprechauns fly?
I really can't say.

But the leprechaun flew
quite a distance that day!

And when he returned,
he was tired and sore.

But the bunny just laughed.
"Oh, you're back for some more?"

The leprechaun strewed Easter baskets all over.

The bunny hid the leprechaun's pants in the clover.

They fought
all that morning

and all afternoon.

They fought
all night long
'neath the light
of the moon.

Then over the hill,
to their great surprise,
flew a giant round baby
with chubby pink thighs.

"Sorry to move all those things in my way, but I'm getting ready for Valentine's Day."

The leprechaun frowned.
"That was three weeks ago!"

Cupid huffed. "I am planning
for *next* year, you know."

And they might've kept
yelling until they turned blue.

But they got an idea—
a *naughty* one, too. . . .

"We'll help you," they said
as they slowly crept near.
"We'll do all the work—
you stand right over here."

And with that, the poor tot
was launched into the sky.
"The nerve of that baby."
They chuckled. "Bye-bye!"

(Now, you know it's wrong
to do that to a baby.
Could they have handled it
differently? Maybe.)

But you'll never believe
how this strange story ends:
The bunny and leprechaun
finally were friends!

(Well, sort of.)

About This Book
The illustrations for this book were
created digitally using Adobe Photoshop
CC. This book was edited by Deirdre Jones and
designed by Angelie Yap with art direction by Saho Fujii.
The production was supervised by Kimberly Stella, and the
production editor was Marisa Finkelstein. The text was set in
Sunbird, and the display type is Balford.